The Grateful Gate

Written by Joy Husted
Illustrated by Grace McKibbin

A Rhyming Story to Inspire 3 to 8-year-olds to have a Grateful Mindset

Published by Once Upon a Rhyme in 2021

@onceuponarhymebooks on Facebook

hustedjoy@gmail.com

© Joy Husted, 2021

Set in Dyslexie Font Pt 16 :B504-4637-69DA-984A-CF7A-081E-6709

ISBN : 979-8-8486-4834-8

ONCE**UP** ON A RHYME

Gates are all around us,
they're common as can be.
You'll probably see a few each day,
maybe even three.

These gates are different colours,
a variety of shapes.
They are the things one opens
when one enters or escapes.

You might not think about them
as you go about your day,
but you're sure to walk right past them
as you run and skip and play.

For Robin, gates are not just gates;
they have a deeper meaning.
They remind her to be thankful
for all that she's receiving.

Robin hasn't always thought
in this unusual way.
In fact, it all began for her
one windy autumn day.

Robin was out searching
in the groundcover and brush
when a quill landed at her feet
from a hedgehog in a rush.

His name was Jeremy
and he was one to grumble,
and right then he was moaning,
'cause his tummy had a rumble.

Jeremy turned to grab his quill
and started to complain,
"It's so unfair, I often lose
parts of my prickly mane."

He carried on complaining
about his very poor eyesight,
"I can only see things clearly
in the middle of the night."

Robin thought about everything
that Jeremy had just said
and soon began to realise
why Jeremy felt such dread.

Robin gently counselled
her cross and grumpy friend
that being a bit more thankful
could help his mood to mend.

BURROW LANE

Jeremy thought about
Robin's kind and wise advice.
He thought it sounded doable
and really very nice.

He had so very, very much
he could be grateful for,
from his soft and comfy bed,
to his fine rug on the floor.

"If I wasn't so forgetful
about choosing gratitude,
then perhaps I could improve
my grouchy attitude."

"Don't worry," said sweet Robin,
"you just need something helpful,
something that you see each day
that will remind you to be grateful."

Jeremy thought about this
and realised something sweet.
Each night he walked through a gate,
to look for food to eat.

"'Grateful Gate' is what we'll call it,"
Robin shouted with delight.
"After a few days of gratitude,
you'll find that I am right."

That night hedgehog returned
from dinner rather late.
He paused to think of something nice,
as he reached his bright red gate.

As he tried to think of something
he could be grateful for,
he saw a new quill poking out
where the old one was before.

Losing quills was not so bad,
and not a cause for moaning.
Old quills dropped and new ones grew,
it simply meant he's growing.

He locked his gate with ease,
his eyesight sharp and clear
and realised that his night vision
was something to hold dear.

This trick he learnt from Robin
was really rather great;
he soon became quite grateful
as he often saw a gate.

You can use this reminder
to appreciate your things.
You'll start to love the happiness
this way of thinking brings.

20

So, each time you see a gate,
there's something you must do.
Remember to be grateful,
and you'll be happy too!

The Grateful Perspective

Gratitude is defined as feeling or showing appreciation for something that is done or received. It entails a shift in focus from the things you do not have to the things you do have. In many ways, gratitude is a fairly abstract concept for children to grasp, especially when faced with competing emotions

such as disappointment or jealousy. However, parents and teachers can model a grateful attitude and outlook on life for the children in their care. As children witness and experience the positive outcomes of a grateful attitude, they will be encouraged to adopt this way of thinking and approaching life. When it comes to gratitude, sometimes we just need a place to start or a simple reminder. The Grateful Gate was written to give children a simple yet fun reminder to think of all the things that they can be grateful for in their lives.

How to Encourage Gratefulness

When modelling gratitude for your child, you should aim to do it in a fun and gentle way. Below are a few fun ideas on how to inspire your child to embrace a grateful attitude:

1. Adopt Jeremy's little trick. Every time that you walk or drive through a gate, shout, "Grateful Gate!" and have everyone think of something that they are grateful for!

2. Take gratitude walks. While walking, point out the little wonders of life and how we can be grateful for them. For example, you may point out the warm sunshine, pretty flowers, or lively bugs!

3. Create a family gratitude jar. At the end of each week, ask family members if they have something that they are grateful for that you can write down and add to the jar. Every three months, make an occasion of reading out all the notes that have been added to the jar.

Hedgehog Facts

1. Hedgehogs are nocturnal, which means that they sleep throughout the day and are wakeful during the night.

2. The average hedgehog has more than 5000 quills/spines.

3. Despite their small legs, hedgehogs can walk remarkably long distances. They have been known to cover as much as 3km in a single night's excursion.

4. A group of hedgehogs is called an array. However, hedgehogs are generally solitary creatures.

5. One reason for the name 'hedgehog' is that they tend to make their homes in hedges and bushes.

Problem Solving and Reflective Questions

1. Can you find the grasshopper on each double spread?

2. How many gates can you find in the whole book?

3. Can you remember what Jeremy was grateful for?

4. Look at the picture on pages 12 and 13, then look away and try to remember all the different items.

5. Can you think of three things that you are grateful for?

Once Upon a Rhyme series

Stories to encourage social and emotional development:

Once Upon an Antelope - Anger management
Once Upon a Crocodile - Learning to embrace differences
Once Upon a Giraffe - Managing stress and anxiety
Once Upon a Hippo - Dealing with loneliness
Once Upon a Hyena - Choosing kindness
Once Upon a Bush School - Celebrating strengths
Once Upon a Recipe - Story for fussy eaters

The Good Reminder Series

Join Lerato the Tortoise as she encounters a Kindness Door and is inspired to start her very own kindness project.

Join Jeremy the Hedgehog in this delightful story as he discovers the trick to having a grateful mindset.

Join Bobby the Bunny as he conquers his fear and learns that even though he is small and feels scared, he can also be brave.

Find out more about these books on Facebook @onceuponarhymebooks

These titles can be purchased in the USA from www.amazon.com as paperbacks or on Kindle (some titles are available on Kindle Unlimited)

Made in the USA
Coppell, TX
13 September 2022